S0-BOG-973

# Geronimo the Frog

10/1/16
TO RONIN,
GERONIMO ROCKS!

By Matthew Stein

Copyright © 2013 Matthew Stein

Illustrations Copyright © 2013 Taillefer Long

All rights reserved.

ISBN: 1482535653

ISBN 13: 9781482535655

Library of Congress Control Number: 2013909992

CreateSpace Independent Publishing Platform

North Charleston, South Carolina

Deep in the heart of the Big Cypress Swamp of Florida lives a brave frog. His real name is Kute, but everyone calls him Geronimo. This is his story.

1

When Kute was just a little frog, he used to swim up to the edge of the Seminole Indian camp and listen to the stories the Native Americans told around the campfire. He loved to hear the tales told of two great Indian warriors, Geronimo and Osceola, who had spent time in Florida long, long ago. Stories of the bravery, fearlessness, and courage of these great warriors had spread around the world.

Kute liked to pretend that he was the great Geronimo. He found an old eagle feather and tied it around his head with a bright red rag he had found floating in the swamp. His favorite game was to hide quietly in a tree, waiting until one of his brothers or sisters wandered by. Then, suddenly, Kute would leap into the air and scream "*Geronimo!*" This terrified his brother and sister, who ran off crying for their mom. There was many a night when Kute's angry mother sent him off to bed without his horsefly stew dinner. Soon all the forest animals began to call Kute "Geronimo."

One day Geronimo's best friend, Echaswa the Raccoon, ran into the clearing all out of breath. "Geronimo, you've got to help us!" Echaswa yelled.

"What's wrong?" asked Geronimo.

Echaswa explained that a gang of thugs, led by Bad Billy, were having wild parties in the park at the edge of the swamp, and that Bad Billy and his gang were leaving garbage all over the place. A lot of this garbage was drifting into the swamp. Their friend Ooeefuswa the Heron had become ensnared with a plastic six-pack ring stuck around his neck and would have choked if Kunu the Squirrel hadn't come to his rescue and chewed it off.

"That's it! We've got to do something about Bad Billy and his gang!" declared Geronimo.

"But what can we do?" asked Echaswa. "They are so big and we are so little."

"I have a plan," said Geronimo. "Go find all your friends. Gather together as many of the forest and swamp animals as you can. Tell them to meet me in the clearing in one hour."

Off ran Echaswa. He found Ooeefuswa the Heron, Loja the Turtle, Kunu the Squirrel, Cesse the Mouse, Yube the Alligator, Obu the Owl, and Koowe the Panther. All the animals were upset about the garbage left near their homes, so they gladly came to the meeting in the clearing. When they heard Geronimo's plan, they all thought it was a terrific idea. Everyone eagerly agreed to help.

The next morning, each animal found a hiding place in the park where Bad Billy and his gang liked to party. They didn't have to wait long for the party to start. Bad Billy and his gang tossed their empty cups and soda cans into the swamp. Gum wrappers, paper plates, and chip bags littered the ground. Geronimo was furious! Croaking as loudly as he could, Geronimo leaped from his perch high up in the mangrove tree. Down he sailed, straight to his target. He landed smack in the middle of Bad Billy's banana cream pie. As soon as Geronimo landed, the other animals jumped out of their hiding places and charged Bad Billy's gang.

Everyone in the gang leaped to their feet! The whole crew was covered with banana cream pie, mustard, ketchup, and other messy gobs of food. Bad Billy and his gang crashed and smashed into each other in their rush to escape. In just a few minutes, all of Bill's gang had cleared out of the park.

The forest and swamp animals settled down for a feast. Geronimo's favorite dish was the banana cream pie. Koowe the Panther liked the hamburgers best. Ooeefuswa the Heron feasted on strawberries and watermelon, while Kunu the Squirrel stuffed his cheeks full of nuts. Cesse the Mouse happily nibbled away at bread crusts and a piece of cheese.

When all the animals had eaten, Geronimo called them together to clean up the mess that Bad Billy and his gang had left. The ducks and alligators rounded up the litter floating in the swamp. The egrets and herons strolled back and forth, spearing napkins and paper plates with their beaks. Koowe the Panther ran all over, gathering bottles and cans with his mouth. Echaswa used his little raccoon hands to help the other animals place trash into the garbage cans. When the cleanup job was finally finished, the animals stood back and admired their work. The park and swamp were clean again! Geronimo thanked them all for helping out. Tired but happy, each animal slowly headed home.

Several weeks had passed, and Bad Billy was getting tired of having his parties ruined. Each time Bad Billy and his gang returned to the park at the edge of the swamp, Geronimo and the other animals were ready for them. Just when a party was getting hot, the forest and swamp animals attacked from their hiding places and frightened Bad Billy's gang away.

One day, after another failed party, Bad Billy called his gang together. "We've got to stop these meddling critters," Bad Billy said angrily. "This was the last party they'll ever ruin!"

"But how can we stop them?" asked a gang member. "Those wild animals scare us."

Bad Billy answered, "I've been watching them, and I've noticed a big frog with a feather on his head. I think he's their leader. When he jumps, all the other animals follow him. I bet if we capture him, the rest of the animals won't bother us anymore."

As usual, the next Saturday morning, all the animals hid themselves around the park. Geronimo stationed himself in the large mangrove tree in the center. Soon, Bad Billy and his gang arrived. Bad Billy winked at his buddies. This time they were ready for Geronimo.

When Bad Billy gave the signal, the whole gang started throwing garbage in all directions. Cans and bottles flew into the swamps. Plates and napkins littered the ground. This was more than Geronimo could bear. He leaped from his branch, croaking "Geronimo!" Down sailed Geronimo, but instead of the frog landing in cake, Bad Billy scooped Geronimo out of midair with a fishing net. The rest of Bad Billy's gang pulled out sticks and bats from under their shirts and blankets. Without Geronimo to lead them, all the other animals were soon frightened away. It was a sad day for the animals of Big Cypress Swamp.

The animals watched from a distance as Bad Billy threw Geronimo into a birdcage and locked the door. Bad Billy's gang celebrated their victory with an extra loud, extra obnoxious party. To top it all off, they left huge mounds of trash everywhere. Hours after the party ended, when they had finished picking up all the trash, the exhausted animals trudged back to their homes. All they could think about was poor Geronimo locked up in a cage.

Back at Bad Billy's cabin, the whole gang made fun of Geronimo. They called him names and laughed at him. Bad Billy said, "You're not so tough. You're nothing without your animal buddies. Where are they now? You're no hero. You're just a slimy little worthless frog."

Little did they know that at that very moment, Koowe the Panther, Yube the Alligator, and Echaswa the Raccoon were watching from the forest, while Obu the Owl soared high above in the sky.

With his keen eyes, Obu saw everything. Koowe let out a low growl, and Obu called softly, "whooo." Geronimo's spirits soared! His friends had not abandoned him! He knew they would find a way to help him escape. Luckily for Geronimo, he did not go hungry while waiting for his rescue. He whiled away the hours by snacking on the swarm of flies drawn to the filth spread around Bad Billy's cabin.

Obu the Owl called a meeting of all the swamp animals. They gathered together in the clearing. "How are we going to rescue Geronimo?" squeaked Cesse the Mouse.

Koowe the Panther announced, "Echaswa, Yube and I have been to Bad Billy's house. Geronimo is locked inside a birdcage. I can scare Bad Billy's gang away, but I will not be able to get Geronimo out of that cage."

"We must save Geronimo," urged Cesse the Mouse, "but how can we do it?"

Obu the Owl flew down from the mangrove tree and announced, "I have a plan." All the animals quickly gathered around Obu to hear his plan.

That night the swamp animals met in the clearing. Cesse the Mouse climbed up onto Koowe the Panther's shoulders for the ride to Bad Billy's cabin. "Is everybody ready?" asked Koowe. "Hang on!" he warned Cesse, as he took off bounding quietly through the dark forest.

Obu the Owl circled high above. With his sharp eyes, he could see clearly in the darkness. All was quiet at Bad Billy's cabin. Everyone was fast asleep. With a "whoo, whooo," Obu signaled that it was safe to proceed.

Koowe the Panther, Echaswa the Raccoon, and Cesse the Mouse quietly crept up to the front door, while the other animals hid nearby to keep watch. Echaswa climbed up onto Koowe's shoulders to reach the doorknob. With his little racoon hands, Echaswa was able to twist the doorknob and let the other animals in. They crept right by Bad Billy's sleeping gang. "Phew, it sure stinks in here," whispered Koowe.

Geronimo was overjoyed to see his friends. "Boy, am I happy to see you," whispered Geronimo. Pointing toward the keys hanging from a beam high above the floor, Geronimo said, "The keys to my cage are hanging over there. I don't know how you're going to get them down, but if you can't, I'm doomed."

Now it was Cesse's turn to help. The little mouse climbed up the wall and then scampered along the top of the beam to where the keys hung. She pushed and pushed, but she could not dislodge the keys from the nail from which they hung.

"I can't do it!" moaned Cesse.

"You must try harder," urged the raccoon. "For Geronimo's sake, you must not give up!"

Cesse thought, "I can't let Geronimo down. I can't give up!" She pushed and strained against the keys. She gave all that her little mouse body could give. Finally, the keys slipped off the nail and fell straight toward Bad Billy. Koowe darted forward and caught the keys in her mouth, just inches above Bad Billy's head. The animals all held their breath as Bad Billy stretched and yawned. They each gave a sigh of relief when Bad Billy rolled over and went back to sleep.

"Phew, that was a close call," croaked Geronimo.

Koowe brought the keys over to the spot beneath Geronimo's cage. Echaswa the Raccoon grabbed the keys in his mouth and once again climbed up onto the big cat's shoulders. Koowe stood on his hind legs and placed his paws against the wall below the cage, stretching as tall as possible to get close to Geronimo's cage. Echaswa had to climb on top of Koowe's head and stretch as high as he could to reach the cage lock with his little raccoon hands.

"Hurry!" urged Geronimo. "Someone's starting to wake up!" One of the men in Bad Billy's gang sat up and yawned a big yawn. He stretched, then rubbed his eyes. Just as Echaswa unlocked the cage, the man realized what was going on.

"Wake up! They're escaping!" the man yelled, but it was too late. Geronimo leaped from his cage and landed squarely on Koowe the Panther's back, right next to Cesse the Mouse.

"Hang on!" commanded Koowe. "Let's get out of here."

The members of Bad Billy's gang jumped to their feet, colliding with each other as they scrambled to get out of the panther's way. "Not so fast," snarled Bad Billy, standing squarely in the doorway and holding a baseball bat. Koowe paced back and forth in front of Bad Billy. He snarled and growled at Bad Billy. It looked as if all was lost. The animals were surrounded and trapped, with Bad Billy and his bat blocking the only way out. Suddenly, Ooeefuswa and a couple other herons swooped down from the sky and dived at Bad Billy's head. Next, Kunu the Squirrel leaped onto Bad Billy's head and latched onto his face. When Yube the Alligator charged through the door, right between Bad Billy's legs, Bad Billy fell over and the rest of the gang panicked.

"Now's our chance!" squeaked Cesse. "Go for it!" Koowe and Echaswa bounded over Bad Billy and scrambled out the door. All the animals cheered when they saw Geronimo. Mission accomplished! When Bad Billy and his gang dashed out of the house with terrified looks on their faces, all the swamp animals laughed and laughed. Yube the Alligator marched triumphantly out the door onto Bad Billy's front porch. In his jaws, Yube proudly displayed the large piece of cloth he had torn from the seat of Bad Billy's pants.

The animals held a jubilant party to celebrate Geronimo's return. The crickets and cicadas chirped and hummed, the bullfrogs croaked, and the birds sang. Everyone had a wonderful time.

Back at his cabin, Bad Billy gathered his gang together. He was furious! Pounding his fist on the table, Bad Billy declared, "We've got to do something about this frog! We're going to fix him for good. We're going to have the biggest, noisiest, messiest party this swamp has ever seen, then we're going to roast some frog legs."

News of Bad Billy's giant party spread like wildfire. Geronimo suspected that it was a trap, but he had a plan of his own. He gathered all the swamp animals together for a powwow. When they heard Geronimo's plan, they all cheered, "Three cheers for Geronimo!"

Echaswa the Raccoon crept off through the woods to the ranger's house. Trooper, the ranger's dog, was sleeping on a rug next to the ranger's bed. This was a very dangerous part of Echaswa's mission. Dogs and raccoons are bitter enemies, and Trooper was known to have killed many a raccoon. Quietly, Echaswa climbed into the ranger's garbage can. Luckily, he found just what he was looking for, a nice fat juicy bone.

Echaswa took this rib bone over to where Trooper was sleeping and laid it on the carpet in front of Trooper, as a peace offering. Echaswa was terrified! When Trooper woke up, he might tear the raccoon into pieces! He thought about Geronimo and how brave he was. He had to be brave, too!

"What? Huh?" mumbled Trooper as he woke up. "You brought me a bone? Mmmm, and it's a tasty bone, too. Thank you. What do you want?" asked Trooper.

Relieved that Trooper had accepted his peace offering, Echaswa quickly told him the whole story. When Trooper heard what Bad Billy and his gang were doing, he said he would gladly do anything he could to help. Eagerly, Echaswa explained Geronimo's plan.

When the day for Bad Billy's party arrived, the swamp was buzzing with activity. Bad Billy and his gang were busy getting ready for the party, while Geronimo and the other animals were preparing a surprise of their own. Geronimo met with all the swamp animals and assigned each one to a different hiding spot around the park.

Geronimo smeared war paint onto each animal's cheeks. "You must be brave," he urged. "Have courage and we shall prevail."

Soon, Obu took off and flew toward Trooper's house. He swooped down and landed in the tree above where Trooper was sleeping.

"Trooper, wake up," he called, but Trooper was fast asleep. "Whoo whoooo!" he called loudly.

"What, who is that?" barked Trooper. "Oh, it's you, Obu. What do you want?"

"Come quickly," urged Obu. "Bring the ranger. Bad Billy's party is starting, and there's not a moment to lose."

Trooper started barking wildly. The ranger came outside. "What is it, old boy?" he asked. "Is there something bad out there? Let's go see what it is." So the ranger put Trooper on a leash and followed him through the forest and the swamp.

44

Back at Bad Billy's cabin, the party grew larger, louder, and messier. Bottles, napkins, cups, and paper plates were strewn all over the ground. When a whole bag of garbage was dumped into the swamp, it was more than Geronimo could stand!

Geronimo leaped from his high branch, croaking *"Geronimo!"* just as loudly as he could. This was exactly what Bad Billy was waiting for. Quickly, he pulled the fishing net from under his shirt. Once again, instead of landing in the middle of cake, Geronimo landed right smack in the middle of Bad Billy's net.

"I'll fix you, you slimy little frog. You're not going to get away this time," sneered Bad Billy. When Koowe the Panther saw that Bad Billy had caught Geronimo, he bounded across the clearing toward Bad Billy. Bad Billy just smiled and waited for the big cat. Koowe had nearly reached Geronimo when Bad Billy pulled a string and a large net jerked the big cat up into the air.

Koowe roared, but there was nothing he could do. He was trapped just as surely as Geronimo.

Yube the Alligator rushed into the clearing to save his friends. Geronimo cried out, "It's a trap, go back!" but the brave alligator would not turn around. He just could not abandon his buddies. When Yube was about to tackle Bad Billy, he fell into a hidden hole in the ground. Now Yube was trapped, too. Geronimo's heart sank. None of the other animals were big enough, or strong enough, to save him!

"Now we're going to have a wild party, and no stupid frog is going to spoil our fun," sneered Bad Billy.

"No, you're not!" came a voice from the bushes. The ranger jumped out and slapped a pair of handcuffs on Bad Billy's wrists. "You are under arrest for poaching! This panther and alligator are endangered wildlife species."

Geronimo's plan had worked. Not only would Bad Billy and his gang never bother the swamp animals again, but also the judge sentenced them to 30 days of public service. For the next month, Bad Billy and his gang had to work hard all day picking up garbage and litter.

The ranger awarded Geronimo a Medal of Honor and proclaimed him an honorary Seminole warrior with special duties to guard and protect the swamps and forests. These were duties and honors that Geronimo proudly accepted! And to this day, in the Big Cypress Swamp of Florida, you will find a courageous frog with an eagle feather tied to his head. If you should dare to set foot in his swamp, you had better respect and cherish this sacred place, or else face the wrath of Geronimo the Frog!

## THE END

26228085R00034

Made in the USA
Charleston, SC
31 January 2014